Thumper
Finds a Friend

Printed in Singapore

First Edition

10 9 8 7 6 5 4 3 2 1

Library of Congress Cataloging-in-Publication Data

Driscoll, Laura.
Thumper finds a friend / by Laura Driscoll; illustrated by Lori Tyminski, . . . [et al.].—1st ed.
p. cm.
Summary: With a little help from his father, Thumper the rabbit learns
how to make friends with a shy hedgehog while playing tag with his sisters.

ISBN-13: 978-1-4231-0437-7 (hardcover)
ISBN-10: 1-4231-0437-4
[1. Friendship—Fiction. 2. Tag games—Fiction. 3. Rabbits—Fiction.
4. Hedgehogs—Fiction.] I. Tyminski, Lori, ill. II. Title.
PZ7.D79Thu 2007
[E]—dc22
2006026424

For more Disney Press fun, visit www.disneybooks.com

Thumper Finds a Friend

by
LAURA DRISCOLL

❧

illustrated by
LORI TYMINSKI, MARIA ELENA NAGGI,
GIORGIO VALLORANI & DOUG BALL

DISNEP PRESS
New York

Under the warm, bright summer sun,
Thumper and his sisters played tag in the forest.

One bunny chased and one bunny wriggled,
one bunny ducked and one bunny giggled,
and one bunny dove for cover . . .

. . . and discovered someone who was trying not to be found.

"Hello!" Thumper said. "Want to play tag?"
The hedgehog stirred and started,
then stumbled and tumbled.

But she didn't answer.
Instead, she tucked her head down
and rolled herself into a prickly little ball.

Thumper was puzzled.
Didn't she want to be his friend?

Maybe he could make her laugh.
He looked for something soft and tickly.

Flick, flick, feather-flick.
The hedgehog giggled, but Thumper didn't hear.

Then Thumper had another idea.
He would give her something sweet!
Skippity-skip, skip, skip.
He hopped to a berry patch
and picked some treats.

Thumper put some berries
next to the hedgehog and waited.
But she was silent and still.

Thumper was stumped.
Didn't the berries smell good?
Didn't they taste good?

Sniff, sniff . . . gulp!
Yes! They were delicious. . . .
At least Thumper thought so.

But the hedgehog still hadn't said anything.
Thumper didn't know what to do.
He hopped over to his father.

"Papa," he said, "why won't the hedgehog be my friend? I've been really nice."

Papa Bunny smiled. "Not everyone makes friends right away. Give her a little time," he said. Thumper nodded and hopped over to his sisters.

Thumper and his sisters scampered and chased.
They darted and they raced. . . .
But still no hedgehog.

The bunnies jumped and joked.
They leaped and they laughed. . . .
But still no hedgehog.

Lots of time had gone by.
Thumper crept toward the tree.
"Want to be friends?" he called.

But the hedgehog was gone!
GONE?

Then Thumper heard a small voice.
"Hello," it said. "May I play?"

So that afternoon, under a warm, bright summer sun,
five little bunnies and one little hedgehog
played tag in the forest.

The hedgehog chased,
while one bunny wriggled and one bunny slid,
one bunny giggled and one bunny hid,
and one bunny smiled . . .

. . . because he had made a new friend.